HAVE WE MET?

IVY GEORGE

ISBN 978-1-68509-949-7

To my dreams and the voices inside your head

Contents

The Bar

She adorns herself with jewelry borrowed from the stars, her sultry lips stained her wine glass, and her eyes sought for trouble. She wore Dele, choking the air at the bar. Regret, long gone out the back door, mischief knocking on the front door. The bar caressed a lonely Lora, switching between wine and vodka, falling prey to the young night. The shifting eyes at the bar made it seem like they all wanted to take her home. A couple of shot glasses away, Darren noticed a young lady, desperately trying to make a conversation with a businessman. He couldn't help but notice Lora at the counter, her body, present, and her mind drenched in memories of a happier past, talking to a man in a suit. The laughter did not summon her mind that lingered around what seemed to be a painful memory from the past. She looked away for most of the conversation, traveling to places in her mind. Perhaps, someone had passed away in her family and she's drinking away her pain, or she could be the rebel who listened to her boyfriend more than her mother. Perhaps, she might be someone who thought spending the night with a stranger was the best way out of whatever she felt. Her lips told tales of time to the man, but her eyes were trying to show him the exit. Lora sipped her free drink and pretended to be interested in business talk. Eventually, their glasses ran out of beer, words ran dry and Lora was sitting across the counter with her hand on her chin. A businessman, so, not her type, Darren thought to himself. He took his glass of beer and went to her.

Is this seat taken? He asked, looking at the empty chair beside her.

Maybe, she replied, are you going to buy me a drink?

Glad you asked, Darren exclaimed. He turned to the bartender and said "One martini for the young lady here, please! "

Lora's hand still holding her chin in place, looked as though she could never come back from where she'd been.

"So, you work around here? asked Darren

"I work at the Lemuel Bookstore" replies Lora.

"You must love reading, I suppose"

"That's true, I admire the way words always find their way to cling onto each other. Words that make sense, of course. Otherwise, it would be utter chaos. As if the world isn't in much chaos itself." says Lora.

Here's your drink, Madam, said the bartender.

"And do you have a favorite?" asked Darren.

"You know what I find interesting?" She gulps down the martini and stares into his blue eyes. "Words don't only serve the purpose of communication. When someone talks, words don't just roll out of their mouths, they are always calculated to either hurt or to win something or someone never meant to confuse. They know exactly what they mean when they say it. I just broke up with Martin whom I thought was the one. "

"Oh boy! What have I done?" Darren thought to himself. He looked into her eyes, filled with tears, lost in a world that she had created for her and Martin.

"How stupid of me to think that being together for 7 years eventually would end up being "till one of us dropped dead". A tear rolled down her cheeks and down her palm placed under her chin. "And boy, did he have a way with words! He knew exactly what to say. Why would someone say all those things and the next day, pretend like they never meant it? Like he said, all those words just for the sake of saying it. What happened to "being honest"? Why couldn't he just be honest with me, after all these years?" Lora chuckled. "Guess, He really did want to hurt me." Lora's blurry vision saw every moment of bliss flash in front of her eyes. Darren watched as he felt the urge to hug her but held back as he was just a stranger at the bar. "However, words will tell you what you ought to know, not time, not experience, not a pat on the back, and not looks across the counter.

"I do think you are one to look at", said Darren. Darren looked at the starry-eyed woman."

"And here I am", she raises her glass of martini and says "trying to forget him with a martini," Lora choked on her words, "even this drink reminds me of him. Martin, martini, and what do I get? men in suits trying to hit on me all night." Lora let her tears run wild on her cheeks.

"Think of a joke, Darren! C'mon, hurry, a joke. Something to get her mind off that memory!

"I am such a failure', Lora exclaimed. I could have done better! I've got to go. It's late and thanks for the drink."

Lora left the bar and Darren in awe. Nothing seemed to replace the way she felt about Martin. "Words can tell you how not to hurt a person," Darren thought to himself. Something about her sought an eerie vibe that got the best of me. I had to see her again. Not that it meant anything, just to find out if she's doing alright. And I didn't hesitate to go up to Lemuel's bookstore to get a glimpse of her. Maybe I seemed right to talk to, maybe all she wanted was a hug, or a shoulder to cry on or rant about how she'd lost the one thing she felt worth living for. The next sober morning was Monday and I hadn't forgotten the way she looked at the bar lights that hid her tears, the stroke of her palm on her tears, the way her hair played between her fingers, the Dele that replaced the sweaty bodies and a drink that spoke a hundred words.

Darren lived on 54th East Avenue, just a couple of blocks down from the Lemuel Bookstore where Lora had worked. He was never fond of the early morning bustle and therefore resorted to working only night shifts at the gas station. Henry admired his perks, mostly because he had agreed to work every night and seldom creeped out the customers unlike Jimmy, who at the first sight of a female figure would flip like a coin tossed into the air. Darren wouldn't have to deal with any of his co-workers except on payday, where the boys hung out at the local bar, drank beer, and talked about stories of how they were tipped by high-functioning women who think they have figured their way out in this world. Their trivial conversations always ended with how Henry's wife left with their dog for someone who worked for him. Sure, Darren laughed but he couldn't care less. You see, it's exactly because of conversations like these that he preferred working night shifts. He wouldn't have to deal with the pain of having to pretend like he was a part of their talks. Darren lived in his mind more than in the real world. The streets of Colorado, his house, his holidays, his mama were so much brighter in his mind than where his body lived. Oh, how he would give anything to hold his mama again. Methamphetamine ran the streets, but never in his veins. The colors were real, and they painted his mind with a picture of a new visitor, Lora. Lora walked through lonely lanes, looking for Darren, searching wide to see his face, to hold his hand and never let go. She would take care of him and love him unconditionally. There would be people who'd look at them and wonder, how can someone be so happy? The children would gather around her, as she told them fables at the corner of Baldwin Street. Darren seemed to have known her for ages and loved every silly detail that made up his world.

Half past 10 in the morning, Darren finds himself at the doorstep of Lemuel Bookstore peering in to find that familiar face. He couldn't see her. He walks into the smell of prints on paper, wood, canvas, and the sound of wind chimes. Emotional wordplay, war times, the sting of love, jealousy, murder, lust, temper penned by a soul who may have looked forward to fame and glamour, on to papyrus, glued to unflawed edges, covered in judgment and criticism. Words, a powerful tool proves to be an age-old weapon to kill and defend the unseen, the unheard, and the unloved. It got me thinking, can a person never love and live unloved? What if no one ever loved Lora?

Amidst the shelves that seemed to stretch a mile, a ray of sunshine from the top window fell upon a flushed face. Lora was trying to arrange the MacGyver series onto the top shelf. Darren took a book from the top shelf and pretended to be reading. He looked at her from the corner of his eye. He was careful enough to not look like a stalker, hence the plaid shirt. According to Darren, stalkers wear black and a cap.

The bookstore was quiet, and the customers seemed to be endorsed in reading the latest arrival- The Widow's stockbroker, by James Hayden. It was about a rich stockbroker who fell for a widow at the coffee shop. He married her and took in her 2 children, aged 4 and 6. Five years later, the woman kills him and buries him in his own house. She files a missing case report and the entire state of California searched far and wide for the missing stockbroker. With no lead, no evidence, no CCTV footage, the case was closed after 2 years of rigorous efforts. She became the sole owner of his entire wealth according to the State Law. She still sleeps on the bed beneath which she had buried her husband. Years later she got diagnosed with a terminal illness and on her deathbed, confessed to murdering her husband.

There were a lot of theories running rampant on the plot. Why had she done this? They seemed to be so happy together. Was it only for money, or was he a horrible person to her? What would have been possibly going through her mind when she picked up that knife?

"You're holding the book upside down, said Lora.

Darren looks on the front cover" Oh!", he exclaimed. Darren stared into her deep green eyes and remembered them differently from the teary ones. She had worn florals and the Dele diffused from her shoulders. Her hair was tied in a bun and she looked hungry. Should I take her out to eat, or would that seem weird?

"Hey, I remember you. You were at the bar that night," said Lora. "Are you following me?"

"No, I just wanted to make sure you were doing okay", Darren replied.

"Now why would you want to do that?" asked Lora.

"Because you seemed really sad that night at the bar, you know, with the whole Martin thing, Darren replied"

"No! I do not want to hear that name! said Lora. The ship has sailed on that one", she says, trying to arrange the second shelf with the Gallagan series. Her hand-carried 4 books, supported by her chest as she kept them in order.

"Oh, I remember! exclaimed Lora, after she had kept the last book onto the shelf. You were the guy who kept looking at me from across the counter while I was talking to the suit" said Lora.

Darren kept the book he was holding back onto the shelf and looked embarrassed. Eye contact seemed to be a little too creepy now. "Oh, did she see me staring at her", he thought to himself. Darren did not know what to say.

Lora widened her eyes "Oh no!". It looked as though Lora had seen a ghost, or came to a revelation, or just recognized who I was.

"I remember telling you everything, the whole Martin thing! exclaimed Lora. "I am so sorry for going on about myself like that to a stranger I met at the bar. You must think I'm stupid and clingy. How did you find me?" asked Lora. "Oh, I'm Lora", she says, reaching out her hand.

Darren reaches out his hand, "Great to meet you", said Lora. Before Darren could say anything, Lora asks him to accompany him to the farthest corner of the library and points to an entire collection of the Huckle brothers.

"They write the best crime novels in the world. There was this one book, where the murderer was committing murders in his sleep and he never knew it."

Darren widens his smile and looks all the way to the top of the shelf and then at her. She kept staring at the collection and talking to me, about how each of the crime thrillers was different from the other, how the Huckle brothers never missed a detail and put in carefully calculated murderers in their plot that no one would even anticipate the real killer. All I could think of was how her hair fell over her forehead, how her fingers ran down the corners of the book while she explained how the Huckle brothers themselves had killed before, how her eyebrows moved in excitement. How can so many facial expressions fit in one sentence?

"Hey!" Lora said snapping her fingers, summoning Darren from his colored thoughts.

"You seem hungry, do you want to grab a bite? asked Darren, I know this good steakhouse, just around the corner. "

Lora squints her eyes and looks at Darren. "Oh, I'm Darren," says Darren, hoping she'd join him for lunch.

"That's a pretty name. Darren, but I don't eat steak" Lora replies.

"How about Thai?" Darren asked.

"Sure", Lora replies.

"It's 1 PM, do you want to go now? "asked Darren.

"Sure! Hey, Lisa", she called the woman who sat at the register, I'm going for lunch.!"

Lisa mouthed "OK", as she held the phone to her ear and polished her nail.

Darren and Lora walk out the door together and as the wind chimes settled Lora looked at Darren and said, "You seem like a good listener, and Thai is a really good option."

As they walked down Norman street to get Thai, Lora turns to Darren and asks," You never told me how you found me".

"I never had the chance. Darren replies

Lora chuckles." I'm sorry, I talk a lot!", well, now you do!

"You told me you work at the Lemuel Bookstore, the night you cried your eyes out," said Darren.

"Of, course. I couldn't be more embarrassed," said Lora.

"It's okay to cry when you lose something dear to you," Darren replied.

"Have you lost something dear to you? asks Lora."

"Mama", replied Darren

"I'm so sorry. I know it's not the same, but you must have felt worse about yourself after she left", said Lora.

They took a turn at the Quinton Alley to a Thai corner. The streets were loud and boiling over with children playing with sticks, men, and women shouting over the hot oven, art dealers looking for a hoax, teenagers fighting over who could pick the bicycle locks the quickest.

I looked at Lora, and it seemed like she belonged here. She looked like she belonged everywhere, and everyone seemed to know her. She belonged to the books, to the alleys, to the sun, to the Huckle brothers, to the martini, and fit perfectly well in his mind, where he would never see her cry again. Lora's eyes widened to accommodate as many wheels in motion as they could. She caressed the dreamcatcher, blew the trumpet held by an old-timer which she then gave to me to give it a try, threw eggs at the local school along with the students. Lora seemed different, fearless, and not the girl I saw cry at the bar.

They talked about how Darren only took night shifts at the gas station, which she found "absolutely ridiculous".

Darren and Lora laughed at Henry's unfortunate life as they gulped down tall glasses of Cha Yen.

"OK, so I'm working one night, and this man in a black leather jacket pulls up to fill the tank. He rolls down the window and hands me a 20 dollar bill. He further asks if I'd known someplace where he could buy firearms. I said, "I don't know, maybe a couple of blocks down the road, there's Willys, you may find what you need there." The man said thank you for the gas and rolled up the window and left. The next morning, I take a look at the front page of the newspaper, and there he was. Right on the front page. I recognized his face. He had apparently shot himself on the head and left a note. And do you know why he made the front page?" asked Darren.

Lora replies "no, why?".

"Because he was the former football legend, Langdon May," said Darren.

Lora gasps, "No way!" She takes a huge gulp of her drink.

"Yep, that was him!" says Darren.

"Are you telling me that you were the last person to see Langdon?", asks Lora

Darren replies "No, that would be the guy whom, he bought the gun from, or if he had stopped at another gas station. Or yea, me."

"Did you tell anybody, like the police or the news?", asks Lora.

"And get more attention than Langdon? No way. Although I do wish I had asked him why he wanted to buy a gun. I had a feeling that he would tell the truth. Maybe he was heartbroken like you." replies Darren.

Darren points a finger at her and says, "No killing yourself over Martin okay?"

Lora laughs and says, "oh he is not worth dying for, I guess. 7 years and that guy just walks out of my life like nothing ever happened. I'm glad I'm over it"

"Tears, reminiscing, and vodka will do the trick I suppose?
asked Darren.

"Funny, genius."

They talked about how Lora's landlord would always
pester her about the rent, even if she were late by 6 hours.
About Nicky, Darren's pet dog who died when he was little.
Nicky was his only friend and when he died, Darren cried
for 2 days. Lora talked about her stamp collection that she
sold to Mr. Hampshire, to send her dying neighbor kid to
Disneyland.

"Darren", said Lora," do you want to do this again? Maybe
have another dinner?"

"Yeah, I'd love to, said Darren.

"Great, tomorrow at 7 PM, pick me up at 108, Lexington
street, said Lora.

Darren felt everything at once, and it seemed like Thai had
bought all the right words sewn into a conversation that
did not turn out to be awkward for either of them. He
called up Henry and asked if he could buy some time for
the following night.

Darren goes into his office at noon to meet him

"So, Is it a girl? Or does your dog need to see the vet?"
asked Henry.

Darren chuckled and said, "I don't own a dog."

Henry casts a doubtful look on Darren hoping he let the cat out of the bag.

"Fine! Her name is Lora," said Darren

Henry's grin widened a mile. He drew close to Darren and pat his shoulder.

"Aye, lad! I knew there was someone out there for you and I bet she's just like you," said Henry.

"Uhm, I may have to disagree on that thought," said Darren.

"You know what, why don't you take the day off. Go on! grab your best shirt and blow her mind away!" said Henry to the wide-eyed boy in front of him.

"Gee, thanks, Henry! See you."

Darren was looking forward to this night. A night where he didn't have to work at the gas station, a night when he didn't have to worry about the change, where he could count the stars with Lora and tell bizarre stories of the customers that come by. The night sky would compliment her smile as I lean in to kiss her. Maybe this is how I find something worth living for.

Meanwhile, Lora was returning from yoga class and she meets an old friend on the way back to her place on Lexington street.

"I cannot believe my eyes if it isn't the wonderful Sally,"
says Lora

Sally threw in a big hug and replied "Lora! I haven't seen you in forever. Where have you been? Come on, let's talk in the café."

Lora and Sally were together from kindergarten till Sally had to move to the suburbs at 5th grade. They were neighbors and went to the park together every Sunday and shared a common enemy, Marley Sanders, the boy who pulled their ponytails whenever they came to the playground. They had years and years to catch up on, and it wouldn't end over coffee. Sally went on and on about how her Jake would always choose to chew on a sour lemon than grapes.

"Aw, that's so sweet," says Lora.

Sally laughed and said "the grapes not the lemon"

So, tell me, Lora, is there a man? asks Sally

"Maybe," said Lora

"Did you guys go out?" asked Sally

"Well, tonight, yes," replied Lora

"Is he cute?" asked Sally.

Lora chuckled as she said, "maybe, he's a really great guy."

"So, it's nothing serious?" asked Sally

"Well, I'm not one to jump to conclusions. I have my assumptions and I'm just letting the waves take me where it leads. And if a storm is headed my way, then I'll try to swim against the current. And if I drown, well, at least I would have tried to be a good swimmer", replies Lora.

"I knew you'd always come up with some old man's saying. Anyways, good luck for tonight. Give me your number, I'll text you tonight, or maybe tomorrow morning, says Lora. Sally winked as she turned to the front door. "Don't do anything I wouldn't"

Lora smiled and she waved goodbye to Sally. She looked at her watch and said, "Oh drat! Its 6'o clock. She hurried to her apartment and took the quickest shower ever since the summer midterms.

Date night

Lora decided to cook dinner for the night. She made ravioli with grated parmesan and baked a raspberry pie. Lora knew she'd surprise Darren with dinner and candles. She made sure her dining area looked homely and decided to dress up for the evening.

"Well, hello there, wardrobe, and dresses I haven't seen since Jillian's wedding," said Lora as she runs her fingers through silk, satin, wool, red, pink, green. Picking out an outfit for the night seemed to be next to impossible.

"Ah! There you are," said Lora, "you look like you could do some good today. She picked a black dress and silver jewelry to go with it. She wore red gloss and let her hair play around her shoulders. She wore heels that could kill, with desires to fulfill and every little detail of the night would play in sync to the melody that tunes their words, their smiles, their inhibitions.

Darren arrives at 108 Lexington street and rings the doorbell. Lora runs to the door and Darren could hear her footsteps on wood. She opens the door to a young man in faint blue, his hair slicked to the side and a smile that made her looked to the ground. Innocence had no room between the two and their widened eyes said a million words in seconds. Darren seemed to be contained, but nervous.

The two of them looked at each other and said "Wow"

Darren laughed and said " well, I said it first"

Lora smiled.

"You look stunning!" says Darren.

Lora says "Well, you don't look so bad yourself."

"Flowers are cliché and don't go well with my blue," says
Darren

"Funny, Come on in. I've got some wine," says Lora

Darren goes inside her apartment. He looks at the photos
on the mantle where Lora's childhood photos were kept.

Darren pointing at a photo of Lora in a jersey, holding a
hockey stick said to her, "So, Hockey?

Lora pours 2 glasses of white wine in the dining room
where she could see Darren pointing at the photo.

"Yes, only because dad insisted, replied Lora "He was a big
fan of it."

"I was more drawn to ballet than boots that make your
feet smelly," she said pointing to the photo of her posing as
a ballerina." My instructor said that I was a natural." She
hands him the glass of wine and heads to the couch. "Dad
would always tell me that hockey is for strong girls and
ballet for the weaker ones.

"Well, it's a contact sport. You keep getting injured on the field and that might make you a stronger person?" asked Darren with a tinge of sarcasm in his tone.

Lora replied "maybe". She sips her wine as she takes another photo from the mantle, "This is from when we visited my grandma in Arizona, and she had a horse and she let me ride it."

"Oh, that's good," said Darren

"She used to tell me a lot of stories about Dad and his brother, about how they made a catapult and tried it on Dad. He was so scared but agreed to be a part of their experiment. He eventually ended up with 3 stitches to his forehead." said Lora

Darren smiled as he held the frame and looked at Lora.

"She said I was her favorite," said Lora

"You miss her, don't you? asked Darren

"Very! She passed away in April."

"Oh, I'm sorry, must have been tough on you."

Lora goes into the kitchen and sets a timer on the oven. She lit some candles and began to set the table.

"A little. But it wasn't uncalled for, she had cancer and the doctors gave her a year. I'd send her flowers every day." replies Lora

Darren smiles at her, puts the photo back onto the mantle, and takes a sip of his wine.

"What about your grandparents? Are they still around?" asked Lora.

Lora goes back into the living room where Darren, with his wine glass in his hand, puts back tiny stuffed animals over the mantle and turns to Lora, and walks towards her.

"Um, no, I have never seen them," replies Darren

He peeks at what Lora was doing and looks at her.

"I made dinner!"

"Woah!" exclaimed Darren.

He looks at the table set for two and flowers in the center and says, "This looks wonderful, I mean it even looks prettier than you."

AH!, exclaimed Lora.

"I'm kidding," said Darren with a giggle. "But I thought we were going out."

"I know, I'm sorry. I hope you don't mind," said Lora

"Mind? Not at all. It looks delicious. It's just that you went through a lot of trouble. I would have pitched in if you'd call me." said Darren.

Lora smiled as she said, "oh it was no trouble, I love cooking. Besides, I thought I could surprise you.

"Surprised, I am!" said Darren.

"Why don't you have a seat."

"Sure!, thank you, Lora," said Darren

The pair pull out chairs and sit opposite the other. The aroma of the ravioli filling the air between them and the flowers blocking their view of each other.

"Well, I 'll keep this here," said Darren. He picks the flowers and puts them aside on the table. "I can't really see your face."

"Too much?" Asked Lora.

"Nah! Just perfect," replied Darren.

Darren was surprised indeed. He thought to himself, guess she has a lot of time in her hands.

"So, where were we?" asked Lora.

"Grandparents," replied Darren.

"Ah! So, who told you stories then?" asked Darren.

Darren laughed and replied, "Well, I grew up on a farm and there was this old lady who came to milk the cows."

He cuts through the ravioli and takes a bite.

"This is delicious!" says Darren who was waiting to compliment her on her cooking.

"Thanks. Glad you're liking it."

"I used to sit beside her, and she'd go on and on with her endless stories. She spoke in German, and I did not get one word. But I would stay and listen, just to make her feel like there was someone to listen. She'd cry in between and I'd have no idea why. She would make rifle sounds and I'd figure it was the war times. And when she'd laugh, I'd laugh along with her. I bet if I'd understand, I'd laugh for real." said Darren.

"Did you ever tell her that you never understand?" asked Lora.

"No. Maybe she just needed to vent out. Listening to her rant was the best part of the day. You know, she was my inspiration to take German as my major". replied Darren.

"How old were you then?" asked Lora.

"10 or 11 years," Darren replied. "If I see her again, I'd speak to her in German and probably tell her the truth about our one-sided conversations, where she kept going on and I would just pretend to understand. Poor Aunt Helma!

"She wouldn't probably recognize you."

"At least, I'll know how to tell her," said Darren. Where did you learn how to cook?

"Grandma," replied Lora. "She cooked a great deal and she used to keep a book where she wrote all her recipes down and drew how they would look like.

"She'd draw them?" asked Darren, staring at Lora.

"I know it sounds silly", replied Lora. "But she made sure they look and taste exactly like how she made them the first time."

"It's not silly at all, I think she's interesting," said Darren.

"I made her favorite dessert for tonight, Raspberry pie".

"Sounds wonderful, Lora."

They go on to talk about how Lora would return to school on her bike and cross Mr. Pauly, who owned a ridiculously loud lawnmower. The neighbors would yell at him, the minute he switches on the lawnmower and refuse to turn it off. Darren enjoyed how Lora's laugh would sound like a tea kettle going off. It seemed like every word the two said knit their lives onto each other's minds, painted them all sorts of colors, and pretended to be in each other's scenarios. Lora was right along with Darren when he got scolded by Mrs. Dorson for not tucking in his shirt in 7th grade. Darren was right beside Lora when she got her first ear piercing on her 18th birthday, holding her hand as she screamed at the top of her lungs. When she won the championship for hockey in high school, Darren was with her, cheering her on.

Lora suddenly remembers a detail and asks Darren, "do you have to work tonight?"

"No, Henry gave me the day off. I'm good for the night" replied Darren.

"Great, it would suck if you left. And I'm glad you're not in a suit, Darren"

"I knew how you felt about suits," said Darren. That night at the bar, I saw you rolling your eyes at a businessman in a grey suit, pretending to be part of his conversations."

Lora gasps and says, "I knew it, I knew you were staring at me. Besides, that man went on and on about how his colleagues would push him around in the office chair with wheels when his boss wasn't around."

"Well, that sounds fun," said Darren

"Till, he was rolled right into his boss's office and was left there by the same colleagues who pushed him around for fun.

"Ouch!"

"Apparently, he barged in on an official meeting with the CEO of Bakers Company," said Lora

"That ought to sting," said Darren

"And that was the day he got fired and came straight to the bar."

"And you broke his heart, Lora."

"Martin broke my heart".

"Lisa broke my heart".

"Marley Sanders and I were sworn enemies and I dated him for a while in high school and then I broke his heart," said Lora

"My Dad broke my Mom's heart," said Darren.

"I broke Jimmy Cullen's heart in college," said Lora

Darren sighs and says, "Wow, that's a lot of heartbreaks.

"Tell me about it", says Lora wittingly.

"I've noticed a pattern in my heartbreaks, we never speak what we actually feel. I remember your tear-filled talk that night at the bar. About how we speak one thing and feel another. Then I thought to myself, maybe this is how I did not see why Lisa broke up with me," says Darren

"It's always something around it. The wrong feelings with the right words" said Lora.

Darren laughs and says, "Everyone's afraid."

"Are you afraid?" asks Lora.

"I am", replies Darren

"I'm afraid too. I'm afraid I'll never have the courage to speak my mind about anything. Literally anything." says Lora.

Darren takes a sip of his wine and says, "I'm afraid this entire night will go by with us trying to be someone we're not."

Lora looks at Darren and says "We are all just looking out to be someone other than ourselves. And strangely, that's what keeps us going. We'll have to keep wearing someone else's shoes that don't fit as well as our own."

"We try to be someone else so much so that we forget who we really are," said Darren.

"Oh, how fragile have we become, Darren."

Silence hovered between the two faces, as they both take sips from their wine glasses, looking at each other, and eventually burst into laughter.

"But we can always laugh about it," said Darren.

"Totally worth laughing about," said Lora.

The night seemed perfect and the two enjoyed each other's company. The timer goes off and Lora rushes to take the pie out of the oven. She sets it on the table as Darren helps her with the table.

"Oh, that's alright. I got them," says Lora

"Please, let me do this, this is the least I can do, says Darren with a grin on his face. "I'll do the dishes while you cut out a big piece of that raspberry pie."

Lora returns to the pie and cuts out 2 pieces

"Whipped cream, Darren?" asked Lora.

"Lots!"

Lora smiles at him as she goes to the couch with the raspberry pie. Darren wipes his hands on the kitchen towel, sits beside her, and takes a bite of the raspberry pie.

"Well, I did not expect that," said Darren

"What? Is it bad? Is something wrong?" asks Lora

Darren laughs and says, no, it's really good!

Lora sighs and then bursts out in laughter as she takes a bite of her raspberry pie.

"So, does the pie look like the one your granny drew?" asked Darren.

Lora reaches to the bottom of the counter and pulls out an old book with tattered edges. The book had worn out and looked like it traveled through time and space to end up on Lora's counter. Lora turns its yellow pages and looks for the raspberry pie recipe.

"Let's find out," says Lora

"Yeah"

"There it is, she said pointing to a picture with the writing at the bottom "to my dearest and best, Lora."

Darren takes a look at the recipe and says "yeah! it does"

"Thank you. Hope you liked dinner."

Darren takes a huge bite off the pie and looks at Lora.

"Like? I loved it."

"I'm glad you enjoyed it, Darren."

"Do you want to watch something? she says, holding the television controller in her hand.

"Yeah, why not. Do you have a collection?"

"Yes," replies Lora. "Hold on, let me just get that for you."

She takes the plate from Darren, places it in the kitchen sink, and goes to the top shelf beside the dining table.

"I have some classics, Richie Grant's Lovable, comedy, thriller. "What would you like?", she says turning to Darren, who was already staring at her going through her collection.

"Comedy, do you have any Stevens Saul? Ever heard of "a mile and a half"? asks Darren.

"Oh yes, I have," replies Lora.

She rushes through her neatly arranged Blu-rays and says, "found it!"

"Great!" says Darren. "It's really funny. We're going to have a great laugh!"

Lora puts in the Blu-ray and sits beside Darren as the movie begins to play.

"This is nice. I'm so much more relieved than all the other times I've been on dates," says Lora

"Why would you be nervous? asked Darren

"Because I'd be trying so hard to impress the guy," replies Lora.

"Lora, you're already impressive, with the pie and the candles, you don't have to try. Being who you are is enough to impress anyone and you're not crying."

"You're funny", says Lora, "and yes, I'm not crying. You're fun to be around."

"So are you. I guess this is a win," says Darren.

Darren and Lora watch the movie and laugh hysterically at the part when John fights an octopus guarding a rare diamond, while Clay tries to climb off the ledge to escape an orangutan. Things were taken pretty slow and as the night and the movie came closer to an end, Lora lays her head on Darren's shoulders and the warmth of his shoulders on her head made her feel like it was the right place to be.

The incident

"Hello, 911?"

"Hello, Ma'am?

"Oh great, there's been an accident at Nelson and Crook's street. There's a woman and a man, there's blood everywhere! There's a car toppled over. Two! two cars.

"Ma'am, how many are injured?"

"I can only see 2"

"Ma'am, were you in the accident?

"No, they crashed in front of me."

"Are you near the victims?"

"No no, I'm scared, there's blood everywhere!

"Ma'am, please stay where you are, we are sending help.

"Oh, thank you, please hurry.

The paramedics arrive at the scene at half-past 7, to extricate John Doe and Jane Doe out of the wreckage.

"There's no pulse, commencing CPR, 1 2 3 4"

"Get me a collar, please"

The paramedics stabilize the mangled body and rush to the Kenneth West Hospital.

"Can we establish an IV access, large bore, and rush a pint of the normal saline stat."

"Brandon, take over, get ready to intubate."

"Compressions at 120 per minute"

"Do we have a pint o-neg"

The ambulance swerved through a curve, as they pass the red light at Queens Avenue.

"Rhythm?"

"Asystole"

"Continue CPR"

"Come on guys, we got this, let's try our best"

The ambulance reaches the Kenneth West hospital, and they are rushed in to receive further management.

"Sir, John Doe, multiple injuries to the head, thorax and lower limbs, possible cervical injuries. We're unable to get a blood pressure on him".

"You've got another one coming"

"Sir, same incident, 2 cars crashed on the highway." Jane Doe, right pneumothorax, deformed upper limbs. 80, systolic. Her abdomen is rigid.

"Ok let's alert the blood bank, book an OR, page Dr. Dennis."

"Do we have a pulse?"

"Yes, sir"

"Ok great let's focus on not losing that and let's do this quick"

"Sir, OR 1 and OR 3 is ready"

"Jane Doe, OR 1, John Doe OR 3," says Dr. Sam "and where's Dennis?"

"He's scrubbing in for John Doe, Dr. Sam"

"Great, Let's not kill them, not tonight!

The halls were filled with dry smiles and teary eyes, some waiting for the good news

"it's a girl"

Some waiting for the bad one

"I'm sorry, we tried our best"

Time doesn't move an inch in these halls and comfort runs rampant amidst the sorrow. The bigger picture never told his mother, that he would be diagnosed with cancer, never told her brother that she would walk with a limp for the rest of her life, never told her sister that she can't be on top of the transplant list, never told his mom that he would have to take antidepressants. Puzzles to be solved and decisions to be made by overworked minds and aching muscles seem to fill the air in the waiting room at the hospital.

Half past 11, Dr. Sam scrubs out of the OR 1 and heads to the nurse's station "Our Jane Doe is a 27-year-old female, Lora Grace Delaney, does she have anyone to contact?" asks Dr. Sam to Nurse Ally.

"Right away, sir."

Nurse Ally searches her contacts and finds Mrs. Delaney and tries to call her up.

"Hello, Mrs. Delaney, I'm Nurse Ally, I'm calling from the Kenneth West Hospital"

"Yes, is everything alright?"

"Ma'am, your daughter's been in an accident, could you come to the hospital?

"Lora?" Mrs. Delaney begins to cry over the phone. "Are you sure?"

"Yes, Ma'am"

"Well, how is she?"

Nurse Ally holds the speaker of the phone and turns to Dr. Sam.

"Sir, she's asking her condition"

"Tell her, Lora's in a critical condition, she needs to come right away," says Dr. Sam

"Ma'am, she's in a critical condition, you need to come right away."

Mrs. Delaney couldn't begin to let the news of her daughter's accident set in. She was devastated. Several memories of her little girl flash through her heavy heart, but she had to hold herself together for Lora.

"I need to see her; she says holding her forehead and trying to find her car keys

"I need to see my baby" cries, Mrs. Delaney.

Mrs. Delaney lived in South Dakota when Lora's dad gave in to cancer. His death was hard on her and Lora was the only one who made her sane. Lora's always been around her mother and loved her very dearly. Their taco nights, movie nights, prom, graduation were memories collected by the two to make them smile on a rainy day.

Mrs. Delaney finds her car keys and hurries to meet her daughter at the Kenneth West hospital. Red lights seemed to have eased up on Mrs. Delaney who was driving at 100 miles per hour with teary eyes. She arrives at the hospital and rushes to the emergency room.

"Sweetie?" She barges in crying at the nurse's station

"Can I help you, Ma'am?"

"Yes, please. My daughter's been in an accident."

"Can I know her name?"

"Lora"

"I'll get Dr. Sam for you, Ma'am"

"Oh, okay, thank you."

Mrs. Delaney looks around at the waiting area full of people with faces that are hard to read and traffic of memories.

"Mrs. Delaney"?

"Yes"

"I'm Dr. Sam, chief of surgery, why don't we take a seat?"

"Is she okay? Can I see her?"

"Your daughter's been in a terrible accident, when she arrived, she wasn't breathing and there were cuts and bruises on her face, we rushed her into surgery. She's got a tube down her throat that is helping her breathe" "Is she going to be okay?" asks Mrs. Delaney

"Ma'am she's in a coma, she sustained a head injury and with her condition, we are looking at a very slow recovery, and let's not lose hope"

Mrs. Delaney's eyes were filled with tears and her voice breaks as she holds Dr. Sam's hand and says, "my baby's a fighter, she'll fight this."

"I'm sure she will, she's very strong," says Dr. Sam.

"Well, she needs someone to be with her right?"

"Yes, Mrs. Delaney"

"Can I see her now?"

"She's in the recovery room, she'll be back in her room in an hour" Can I get you anything? A cup of coffee?

"No, I'll be fine. I'm going to wait here for her."

"Ma'am, we're here for you, if you need anything, don't hesitate," says Nurse Ally

"Thank you."

Mrs. Delaney sits by the window and tries to keep herself together. The news of Lora's condition broke her heart and there are many different ways to break someone's heart. As the waiting got longer and the tears sunk deeper, Mrs. Delaney's heart ached to see her daughter's face.

"Mrs. Delaney?"

"Yes"?

"Dr. Sam would like to have a word with you, would you like to come with me?"

"Of course," replies Mrs. Delaney.

Nurse Ally escorts Mrs. Delaney into his office where she waits for him.

"Mrs. Delaney, you can see your daughter now," says Dr. Sam. I just want to let you know again that she's in a coma, she'll not respond to you, or see you, or hear you.

"Dr. Sam?

"Yes?"

"Was anyone else hurt in the accident?"

"Yes, a young man. He's still in surgery"

"Do we know who he is?"

"Dr. Dennis is working his case, I'll let you know as soon as I can."

"Thank you"

Mrs. Delaney moves to Lora, lying lifeless on a bed with tubes down her throat and wires attached to her body. The monitor beeps to her heartbeat and her hand felt cold to touch.

"My poor baby" says Mrs. Delaney as she tries to touch her forehead.

"It's okay now, sweetie." I'm here for you"

She sits beside Lora and holds her hand and looks to the ceiling with teary eyes. She never actually believed in an upper being, but she may have felt a need to talk to someone.

"So, I haven't done this in a long time, but Lora's a good person and she's all I have left . Please don't take her away from me. I need her to live for me. So, if you are out there, can I have my daughter back, please? Her voice breaks as she holds Lora's hands tighter and promised her that she'd never let go.

Darren

"We've got a bleeder"

"Suction, clamp it, please"

"We're losing him, blood pressure's dropping"

"There's no pulse"

"Begin CPR"

"1 2 3 4 "

"I've got the bleeder"

"Blood pressure's back up to 90 systolic"

"Pulse?"

"Present, feeble"

"That's alright, we've got him."

"Dr Dennis?"

"Yes"

"Sir, Nurse Bradley is on the phone, they've identified John Doe, 28 year old Darren James, we've called next of kin. They are on their way from South Carolina.

"Okay, great, Let's make sure Darren sees his family"

"Suction"

Hours pass and Dr Dennis scrubs out of his OR to meet Dr Sam.

"We got him, Sam"

"Coma?" asked Dr Sam.

"Yes"

"The guy almost bled to death"

"Darren James right?"

"Yeah, yours?"

"Lora Grace Delaney, coma"

"Have you contacted anyone?"

"Yes, Mrs Delaney is with her right now." She's in 214

"Darren's going to be in 213" says Dr Dennis

It's hard for their family, you know, they're both young, they have their whole lives ahead of themselves. They have jobs.

"and dogs"

"and hobbies"

"Remind me, what was your hobby again, Dennis, figure skating?"

"Drawing cartoon, Sam"

"Oh yea, I remember them. They're funny, why did you stop?"

"Well, let me see, yeah, time and I weren't really good friends."

Dr Dennis laughs and says "Ain't no better time than yesterday."

"No, there isn't, Sam"

Dr Dennis and Dr Sam walk through the corridor as they talk about Darren and Lora. The night went by as Darren's sister Penelope arrives as the Kenneth West Hospital.

"Darren!", screams Penelope.

Mrs Delaney hears a loud cry just outside Lora's room and tries to look. She sees Penelope crying on the floor with her hands on the door of Darren's room. Mrs Delaney rushes to her and tries to hold her.

"It's okay, dear. I got you."

Penelope held Mrs Delaney close and cried.

"Penelope, I'm Dr Dennis and this is Dr Sam, We're really sorry about Darren. Your brother had multiple injuries to the abdomen and head, He's slipped into coma and it may take a while, but we are all hoping for the best."

Penelope begins to cry as she looks through the window to see Darren on a machine. She enters the room and embraces her brother, trying to wake him up.

"Darren, Darren, can you just open your eyes for one second," cries Penelope. "Dr Dennis?"

"My dear, I'm sorry about your brother."

It was half past 9 and Penelope lays her head on the side of Darren's bed. She closed her eyes and Darren opened his. Darren calls out to Penelope and plays with her. Mama yelling from the kitchen, while Darren and Penelope fight over who's going to get the most gummy bears. Pain knew bounds in her mind as she was the only there to make Darren stronger.

"Dr Sam"? asks Mrs Delaney

"Is that the boy who got into the accident with Lora?"

"Yes, Mrs Delaney."

"Well, how is he?"

"Same condition as Lora, He is in a coma."

"Darren right?"

"Yes"

"Tell me, Dr Sam, Are Darren and Lora going to be okay"

"Mrs Delaney, only time will tell."

"Dear" says Mrs Delaney, caressing her head, "I'm so sorry"

She pulls Penelope closer to her and hugs her, "It's going to be alright".

"Have you eaten anything, my dear?", she asks Penelope.

"No, she replies.

"Come on, let's get you something to eat. There's a cafeteria downstairs." says Mrs Delaney

"Darren?"

"Well, Lora and Darren are not going anywhere, now are they? Lora is my daughter; she's been in the accident too."

"Oh, I'm sorry," says Penelope laying her tear-filled eyes on Ruby. asks Penelope.

"She's in a coma too." replies Mrs Delaney "I'm Lora's mom, Ruby."

Penelope smiles as she looks at Ruby and finds warmth that she longed for ever since she moved away from her family to the suburbs. They make their way though the halls to the cafeteria. The bustle had found its way from the cafeteria to the minds of people waiting on their loved ones to progress.

"Darren used to love mathematics, so I used to make him do all my homework", says Penelope. "He'd figure out some way to solve calculus by watching videos on how to solve them."

"He must be quite smart" says Mrs Delaney.

"Yep, he's the smart one and the favourite one" replies Penelope. "Tell me about Lora."

"Well, she's a feisty one, never gave me peace of mind while she was growing up." says Mrs Delaney. "She's always trying to pick up fights and stand up against boys who try to bully her or her friends."

Penelope smiles as she takes a bite off the cafeteria food.

"Oh, lima beans tastes awful" says Penelope.

"Hospital food. They are not supposed to be of any good, I suppose." says Mrs Delaney

"I thought so, this food and how I feel are the same. Terrible!"

Mrs Delaney grins and asks, "where are you going to stay?"

"I don't know, I came straight to the hospital" says Penelope.

"Well, why don't you come stay with me for a couple of days, at least till Darren improves." says Mrs Delaney

"Oh no, I don't want to be any trouble", replies Penelope.

"Oh, there's no trouble, I insist, Penelope.

"Okay, thank you so much" Mrs Delaney "I'm truly grateful to you."

Mrs Delaney and Penelope decide to go to her house on Christens Street. Home, a safe haven, was a place Penelope had lost touch with at 18. A figure to pamper, a voice to call you, baskets of unfolded laundry, drawings on the walls, could never leave Penelope's thoughts of a fonder memory that blurred away with time. A trip down memory lane bought tears in her eyes. A distant memory of Darren flashed by as she found a poster of Woody Parson, a famous singer on the door of Lora's bedroom.

"I'll run a bath for you, dear" says Mrs Delaney, holding the door knob.

Penelope looked through the books that filled the shelf in the room and turned to Mrs Delaney standing at the door and staring in.

"This was Lora's room" says Mrs Delaney.

"She loves to read; I suppose?," asks Penelope.

"She'd read every minute of the day" replies Mrs Delaney. I would have to hide the torch she used to read under her blanket when I sent her to bed."

Penelope smiles. "She works at a bookstore" says Mrs Delaney.

"Why don't you take a nice shower while I make some tea, alright dear?"

"Yes, I'll be down in 5" replies Penelope

Penelope ran her finger through the books that were on the shelves.

"The Huckle brothers" she said to herself and pulls the book out of the shelf and begins to read through the first couple of pages. She leaves it on the dresser and quickly gets into the shower as she didn't intend on making Mrs Delaney wait or let the tea go cold.

"There you are, dear. Here's your tea," says Mrs Delaney.

"Thank you so much", says Penelope. "You have a wonderful house."

"Well, a house that's quiet will begin to feel old pretty quick and with Lora's dad not being around, I have to find a way to entertain myself with Lora's old photos and home videos."

"Can I ask where Lora's dad is?" asks Penelope.

"Cancer, we lost him 9 years ago" replies Mrs Delaney.

"I'm sorry," Mrs Delaney.

"It's alright, sweetie." Where does Darren work?" asks Mrs Delaney.

"He works at a gas station" replies Penelope.

"I see." says Mrs Delaney

"He has this weird theory on people and chooses to work only night shifts at the gas station", says Penelope after taking a sip of the tea.

"Well, don't we all have theories on people" says Mrs Delaney. Sweetie, take some rest, you've been driving all this way, you must be really tired."

"But Darren?"

"I'll go back and keep an eye on Darren and Lora, why don't you get some rest and I'll come back for you in the morning."

"Okay, Mrs Delaney."

"Goodnight, dear."

"Good night", Mrs Delaney.

Mrs Delaney decides to go back to the hospital to see Darren and Lora. Darren and Lora only spoke to her through beeps on the monitor. The hustle at the corridors died down as patients returned to their beds, nurses administering power nap in a syringe and surgeons scrubbing off after hours of surgery. The silence suddenly made Ruby focus on the monitors that spoke to her and wondered if this was just for a while or forever. Quarter past 2 in the morning, Ruby falls asleep on a chair next to Lora, holding her hand.

Mr. Universe smiles back

"Look, here comes Mr. Planck", says Darren.

"What is he going to do? asks Lora.

"Wait for it, wait for it, there it is.!" Darren bursts into laughter.

"Did you see him do that double flip and land on his back instead of his feet?" asks Darren to Lora.

"Yea! And ouch, that guy must be in a lot of pain" says Lora.

"There's no pain in comedies," says Darren

Lora laughs as she holds on to Darren's arm. An hour into the movie and Darren finds Lora fast asleep on his shoulders and did not wish to wake her. He gently shifted her head from his shoulder to the pillow on the couch. Darren didn't try to wake her up, instead, he put a blanket over her and made her lie gently on the couch while Darren moved to the couch next to her. He turned off the television and looked at Lora, sleeping like a toddler. Darren drew a smile on his face and closed his eyes. His mind colored pictures of Darren and Lora walking down Quinton Alley to get Thai. Darren's caressing the dreamcatcher with her, blowing the trumpet from the old man along with her, throwing eggs at the school along with the kids, doing anything with Lora beside him. He felt he lived a little more with Lora. Darren turned to Lora in the middle of the busy Thai corner and leans in to kiss her. She hesitates and looks at him. Lora slowly begins to smile and kisses him.

"The old man with the trumpet is looking at us", Darren.

"Maybe I look like him when he was younger, says Darren."

"So, are you saying that the old man was an American when he was younger?"

"Well, guess I didn't think this through," says Darren.

Darren and Lora begin to laugh and as they run through the alley and as she held his hand tighter, he knew that she would never let him go.

Half past 6 in the morning, a ray of sunlight made its way into the living room and onto Lora, lying on the couch in a fetal position. She wakes up to Darren's alarm on the phone.

"Darren," says Lora.

Darren suddenly wakes up to Lora's call.

"Lora, what happened?"

"Nothing, did we finish the movie?" asks Lora, holding the blanket closer to her.

"You fell asleep when Mr. Planck stepped on quicksand and I didn't want to wake you, replies Darren, trying to stretch the numbness off his hands.

Lora laughs and says, "I'm sorry I fell asleep, did Mr. Planck make it?.

"Definitely," said Darren.

Well, then why didn't you try to leave? Lora asked

"I figured you may wake up and wonder what had happened last night, and probably arrive at a conclusion that Darren's a jerk and I wanted to be here to make sure that didn't happen" replies Darren. "And Mr. Planck finally manages to steal the diamond"

Lora laughs and says "well, that's thoughtful. I feel like I have already watched the movie, despite falling asleep, Too much wine?"

"Maybe, Coffee? asks Darren

"What time is it?" asks Lora

"It's 6:37 AM, replies Darren, looking at his watch"

"Oh no, I'm filling in for Cara today, I have to go ,

"Oh, yeah sure.

We'll have coffee when you come back? "asks Lora.

"Yes, definitely, I think I'm going to go. I'll text you, replies Darren

"Bye"

"Darren! Wait", says Lora as she tries to run outside after Darren

Darren turns back and says "What?"

"I don't have your number to text you, Darren."

Darren smiles as he moves towards Lora and asks, "Do you have your phone on you?"

"Yeah, here, says Lora handing the phone over to Darren.

"Here you go, drawing a crafty grin across his face.

"Alright, bye, I'll see you around", says Lora.

Lora goes back into her house as Darren shuffles his pocket for his car keys.

The morning traffic really got onto Lora's nerves as she showed up 10 minutes late for work and her boss was not a fan of latecomers. But Darren caved in the whole morning with a paintbrush between his teeth and colors on his fingertips. As her face slowly took form on canvas, Darren's favorite song came on the radio.

Humming to the rhythm, his feet shuffled through the sound of the radio. The birds on the window peered in to see the lunatic's hands in the air, tracing patterns and swaying with the wind chimes. The noise of the world is sieved when he fell in love with a beautiful soul. Lora was the beautiful soul and for the first time in a very long time, the universe looked upon Darren and winked.

"Oh, what's that you say, Mr. Universe? asked Darren cupping his ears to the air.

"That's right, beautiful soul! And I'm in love with her. You see this dance I'm doing; this is going to be our wedding dance." He swirls across the room to the other corner. "And I'm going to hold her in my arms and dance with her all night long. We'll stop for bathroom breaks only. I'll never be tired of holding her or dancing with her, and she'll never let go of me."

Meanwhile, Lora was not having the best time after her boss gave an hour lecture on punctuality.

"Nope, I'm not going to let this ruin my entire day, Lora says under her breath

"Huh?" says Mr. Barton.

"Nothing, Mr. Barton, replies Lora.

"Get to work, then, replies Mr. Barton.

Lora goes to the Huckle brothers rack and slowly whispers in an evil voice, "Maybe you and I could devise a plan to end Mr. Barton once and for all. I mean, I know you don't like him either, He does not stack you under "famous authors"."

"Lora!" yells Mr. Barton from the Sci-fi section.

"Oh, here we go again!, exclaims Lora.

"You need to stack the 12th edition of Mr. Barn's adventure," says Mr. Barton.

"Yes, Mr. Barton."

As Lora was headed to the northeast corner of the store to stack the magazines, a glimpse of "a mile and a half" stumbled across her mind.

"Darren!" I guess I'll text him.

Lora picks up her phone and leaves Darren a text.

"Boss is pissed, stupid Cara, stupid me. Oh, and by the way, it's Lora."

Darren sees the text immediately. "Oh my, she texted! Guess she remembers. Of course, she remembers. Why wouldn't she remember? Okay, she sounds glum. What do I text her back? Something happy, something to get her mind off of it.

"Hey" replies Darren, to the text that Lora sent.

"Hey? That s what you wanted to tell her? You don't want to make her feel better? Stupid Darren," Darren mutters to himself, thinking of so many different texts that could have been so much better than "hey"

"Lora and Cara aren't the only stupid ones, Darren too. Quick, write something better!," says Darren to himself.

"Aw, that sucks, maybe we should anonymously call the Huckle Brothers. Do you want me to come to pick you up for coffee?

"Hahaha, I thought of devising a plot with the Huckle brothers too. Not now, Pick me up by 5?"

"Sure!"

Parallels

Mrs Delaney was sitting in the corridor when Dr Sam decided to visit her.

"How are you holding up, Mrs Delaney?" asks Dr Sam

"Alright, I guess. I mean it's not really the best place to be right now. Lora's stuck, away from home." She turned to Dr Sam and says, "it's been 38 days. Sometimes I wonder whether she can hear me talk to her or Darren", she says turning to the glass window of room 213, "or is she living within her trapped mind, does she go to work in there? Does she meet someone in there? or worse, what if she likes it there and doesn't want to come back?"

Dr Sam sighs, "You have a sense of humour, I guess Mrs Delaney, you mustn't lose hope. You have to be stronger than ever for Lora."

"And Darren," says Mrs Delaney. I have grown to love him too, just like how I love Lora.

"Where's Penelope?", asks Dr Sam.

"Went to deliver some mails," replies Mrs Delaney.

"Hang tight, they are fighters, they'll come back, says Dr Sam as he put his hand on her shoulders.

"Everybody has something to fight for. Some are fighting for equality, some for the upper hand, some for the larger part of the chocolate, and then some are fighting for others. Darren's fighting for you, and I'm sure as hell know that you are fighting for him. That's what you need to know to keep you from losing hope." says Dr Sam.

Tears lost their way down Ruby's cheeks as she chokes on her words "How could I ever live if I lose her? She's all I got."

Dr Sam tried to comfort her, but time and tears were insensitive to her feelings. Ruby took turns speaking to Darren and Lora's, holding their hands, asking what their favourite cartoon was when they were younger, what they thought of the future to be, what they thought of Los Angeles when they would settle down?

Maybe Ruby's words were all that she had to comfort her till Darren and Lora opened their eyes. A quarter past 2 and Penelope arrives at the hospital to see Ruby speaking to Lora. Penelope's eyes were filled with tears as she went inside to meet her.

"They're going to make it, Mrs Delaney."

Darren's shift began at 9 PM and he had plenty of time to catch up with Lora and what went down at work. Darren met the landlady on his way downstairs. Mrs Jackson was always fond of Darren only because he agrees to collect her mail and leave it at the front door so that she wouldn't have to go through the trouble of walking 1 foot to the mailbox. Darren has also agreed to feed her cat when she's not around and run errands for her.

"Oh, my boy, aren't you looking like a million dollars. Lock at that smile. I'm guessing it's a girl." says Mrs Jackson

"Oh, you're making me blush, Mrs Jackson, and yes her name is Lora."

"Thank heavens. My little boy is growing up! Off you go. I'm not going to let you keep her waiting."

"Bye, Mrs Jackson."

He pulled his car around to go to Lemuel Bookstore, to pick Lora up for coffee. Traffic in the city seemed to be thinned out by efficiently working officers.

"Hey, Lora."

"Hello, Darren, how was your day?"

"It's only going to begin, night shift, remember"?

"I do"

"I do, two words I would like to hear sometime soon", says Darren under his breath.

"what?"

"Nothing, let's get you some coffee"

"Yes, please."

"Sweet ride," says Lora, looking at Darren's dented vehicle.

"Thanks, but I'll go to the workshop soon."

"You better"

"So, what went down at work?

"Mr Barton! He had an eye on me all the time"

"That doesn't sound right"

"No", she said laughing at Darren's reply.

"He's all like, "you know better, you should be more responsible," says Lora imitating Mr Barton's voice.

"Oh, man, sounds like a total jerk. He could have just let it be."

"I guess so, but then again, this is not the first time."

"I see", said Darren and looked at Lora peering out the window. Her eyes were squinted, her hair tried to run away from her forehead and her elbow sticking out the window.

"So, what were you up to?" Darren.

Of course, he did not tell her that there's a 5-foot painting on a canvas of her sitting in his living room, because what if that's not the best thing to do right now or worse what if she thinks I'm from creep-fest.

"Just watching TV."

Darren and Lora stop at the drive-thru at Lazzy's café.

"One black and"

He turns to Lora. "Latte," says Lora.

"Lora, do you want to do something, like a movie or bowling?"

"Oh, I know! We could go skating.

"Skating sounds" he looks at Lora with his eyebrows raised, "good"

"Great"

"Here's your order, sir

"Thank you, good day."

Darren takes a sip of his coffee and asks Lora "so, skating eh?"

"Yep, turn around here, just a couple of blocks over, you'll find "Iceland," says Lora.

"Alright, guess we're doing this"

"How long have we got, Darren?"

"What do you mean?"

"Your shift"

"Ah, that! We have about 3 hours till my shift begins at the gas station."

"Sounds great, we'll skate and grab something to eat"

"Yep"

Except Darren missed a tiny detail. He didn't know how to skate. But he couldn't let that get in the way of Lora's happiness. She needed something fun to do. Darren and Lora, with empty coffee cups in the hand, step out in Iceland.

"I love this place," says Lora. "C'mon!, let's go."

Lora grabs Darren by the arm and makes their way to the ring.

"Here, put these on," says Lora, handing him a pair of skates.

Darren puts them on and tries to head to the ring. Lora notices his hesitation to get into the ring when she saw Darren staring at the ice with his hand holding tight onto the railings like a child.

Lora bursts into laughter and said, "I should have known."

"I should have told"

"C'mon, I'll teach you, it's no biggie."

"I'll fall and embarrass myself, Lora"

"Exactly, now grab my hand, Darren" please tell me this is in your bucket list"

Darren had wishes penned down in his bucket list, but skating was not one of them. The kids in his neighbourhood seemed to be a pro at it when they turned 16 years old, only because they hung out after school. Darren hung out with Legos and paint brushes after school and he liked it very much. Those were times spent within distance, with himself, yet not alone, in his mind, yet awake for all to see. There was so much space within himself, kept away, spent away in his mind, but now Lora's filling them up. He'd be holding her hand even when she's not around. Her voice plays on an endless loop and flowers sway to her words.

"Steady, don't look down, said Lora, skating on Darren's side.

"Okay, but don't let go of me, alright," said Darren.

"Nope, I'm right beside you, Darren."

Raspberry pie

"I think I'm going to get a job at the grocery store, Mrs. Delaney," said Penelope "I need something to get my mind straight." A job would keep me occupied and I could help around the house."

"Oh honey, are you sure you want to look for a job? Darren needs his sister, Penelope.

"It's been 2 months, when is he planning on waking up?" said Penelope.

Penelope goes near Darren's bed and tries to wake him up.

"Hey, wake up! Darren, wake up, you've been sleeping for 2 months"

"Dear," said Mrs. Delaney.

Mrs. Delaney could pick up on her frustration. Living with uncertainty is a difficult task to master. Even the strongest of faces and happiest of hearts will fail at coping with long-term haze. Perhaps Darren and Lora were living in uncertainty too. "When am I going to talk to Penelope?" "When am I going to hug Mummy? "When can we go from the hospital?" Maybe they want out just as much as Penelope wants.

Mrs. Delaney ran out of words to make Penelope feel better and it seemed like the comfort of doubt had made her weary. She left to see Lora, leaving Penelope and

Darren to a room full of memories longed to be visited again, tears longed to be forgotten, love longed to be felt and hope, hope that someday Darren and Lora will come back to them.

Penelope held Darren's hand and began to cry "If you could just open your eyes"

"Penelope?"

"Darren!"

"Dr. Sam, Ruby" screams Penelope

"Lora?" screams Ruby.

Penelope and Mrs. Delaney run out of the rooms and look for Dr. Sam.

"Darren opened his eyes, you've got to see this, Dr. Sam!", says Penelope.

"Lora's opened her eyes too"

Darren and Lora were no longer trapped, locked away. Darren opened his eyes to his keeper, Penelope who loved Darren and never left his side. Lora opened her eyes to Ruby, who would give anything to see her beautiful daughter smile. Penelope and Ruby have gained missing pieces of their life. They were lost, lost in a world where the only thing that made sense was immobilized, lay with a paralysed mind and talked through buttons and colours on a monitor. It was as though Penelope and Ruby felt more alive than them.

"Sweetie, Mum's right here," says Mrs Delaney caressing Lora's forehead and looking at her with teary eyes.

"Miracles are not to be underestimated, Ruby," said Dr Sam.

"Thank you so much, Dr. Sam" "I got my baby back."

"We'll run some tests and scans and confirm that she's in good shape, Mrs. Delaney."

Dr. Sam turns to Lora and says, "Hey, there, you're doing really great and we're delighted to have you back. You're a sign of pure strength, you've pulled through the hard times."

Lora and Darren were on their own path of recovery moreover they lit up the lives of those who loved them dearly. Days went by and progress was evident. Their broken bones were mending by technique and divine intervention, their torn flesh was sewn in finesse and their smiles were glued on for gratefulness.

"Penelope?"

"Yes, Darren?"

"There was someone else too right? In the accident?"

"Yes, her name is Lora, she s in the next room. The two of you slipped into a coma"

"Well, did she make it?"

"Yes, she is doing just fine. Mrs. Delaney was kind enough to let me stay with her until you were well."

"And who's Mrs. Delaney?"

"Oh, my bad, she's Lora's mom, Darren"

"Can I see Lora, Penelope?"

"Yes, Darren" Let me just get your wheelchair" Ruby and I were just talking about when you guys would meet."

Penelope helps Darren onto his wheelchair, to see Lora. And as Darren takes a glimpse at her through the window as they go, he saw Lora putting down an edition of the Huckle Brothers and a face that played images of a past that existed only within himself. A familiarity of the unexpected, unknown, unlived.

"Hey Lora," says Penelope, "look who's finally here to see you"

"Hello, Lora, I'm Darren"

"Hey, Darren"

"Have we met?" asks Darren

"I don't know, maybe," said Lora with a smirk.

"I mean, apart from the horrible accident and I'm really sorry for that, Lora"

Lora chuckles and says, "I'm sorry too, I don't remember a thing from the accident, but I feel like I've known you too."

"Some version of me knows you, Lora."

Well, hello there, Darren" says Mrs. Delaney as she enters Lora's room with some raspberry pie. "Here you go, have a slice of pie, it's my mother's special recipe and Lora's favorite.

"Thanks, Mrs. Delaney," said Darren.

"Darren thought he'd meet Lora, so I wheeled him over", said Penelope chewing on a piece of the pie. "Oh, my this is wonderful"

"Here you go, Lora, have some pie," says Mrs. Delaney handing her a plate and silverware.

Darren looks at Lora with a smile and says, "Raspberry pie."

Ingram Content Group UK Ltd.
Milton Keynes UK
UKHW012243130423
420127UK00007B/677